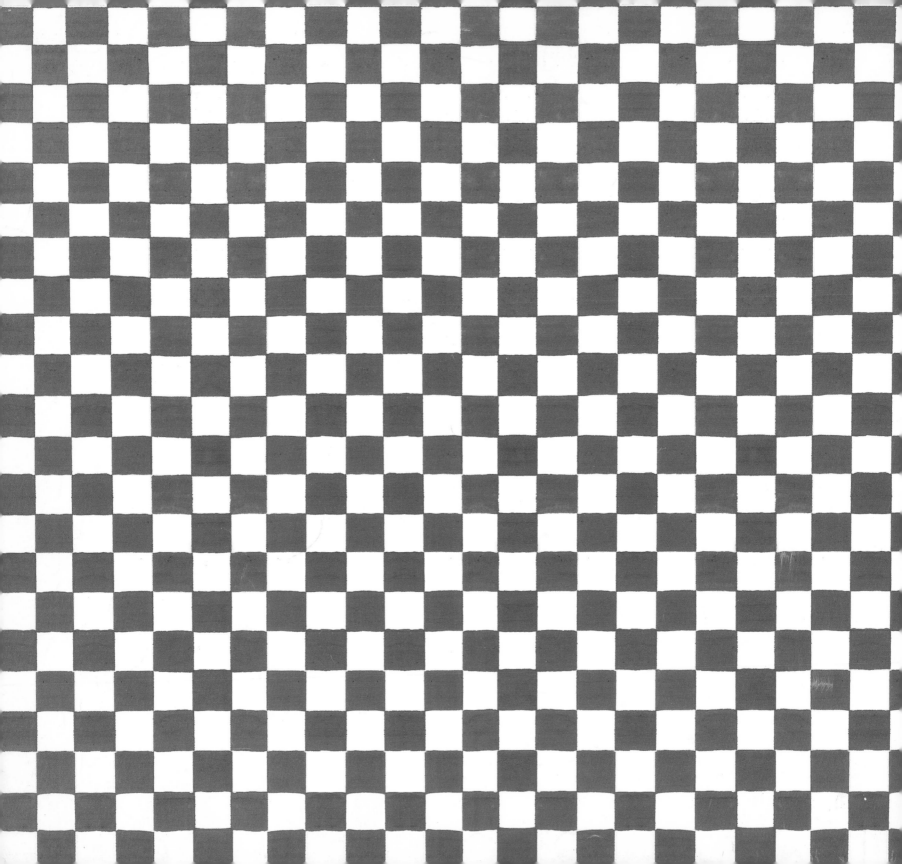

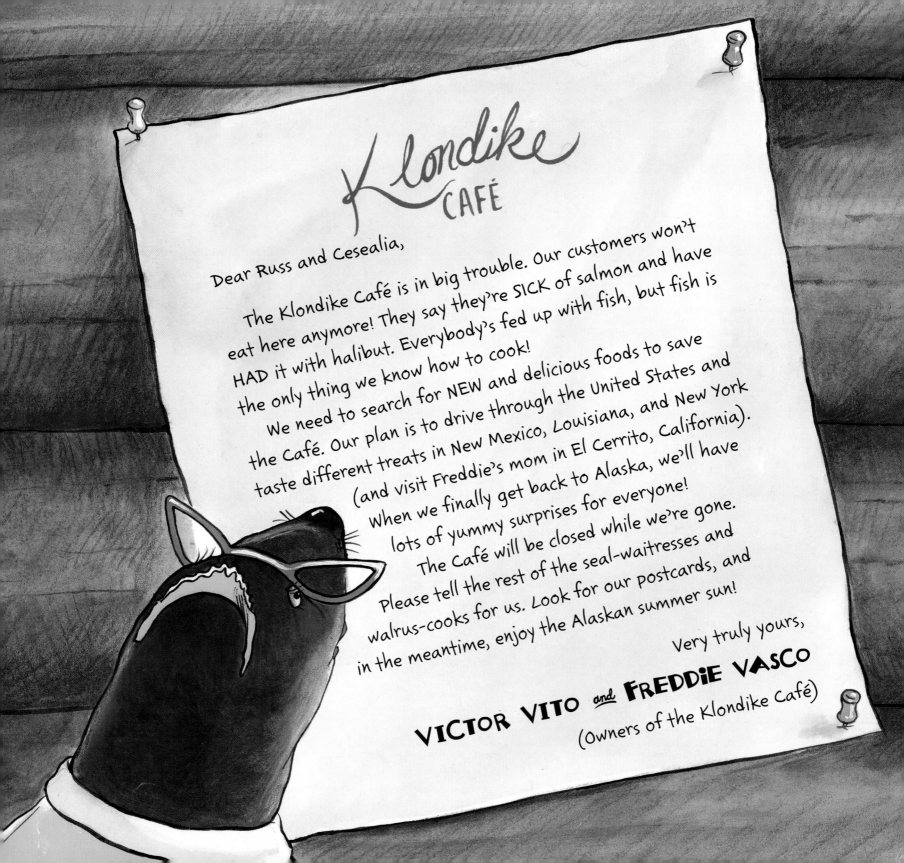

Klondike
CAFÉ

Dear Russ and Cesealia,

The Klondike Café is in big trouble. Our customers won't eat here anymore! They say they're SICK of salmon and have HAD it with halibut. Everybody's fed up with fish, but fish is the only thing we know how to cook!

We need to search for NEW and delicious foods to save the Café. Our plan is to drive through the United States and taste different treats in New Mexico, Louisiana, and New York (and visit Freddie's mom in El Cerrito, California). When we finally get back to Alaska, we'll have lots of yummy surprises for everyone!

The Café will be closed while we're gone. Please tell the rest of the seal-waitresses and walrus-cooks for us. Look for our postcards, and in the meantime, enjoy the Alaskan summer sun!

Very truly yours,

VICTOR VITO and FREDDIE VASCO
(Owners of the Klondike Café)

Getting Ready to Go . . .

ALASKA

NEW YORK CITY

CALIFOR

NEW MEXI

In Louisiana . . .

on their rutabagas,

RAWFISH

VICTOR VITO *and* FREDDIE VASCO ~~moved~~ *drove* from El Cerrito all the way to Alaska.

1 NORTH

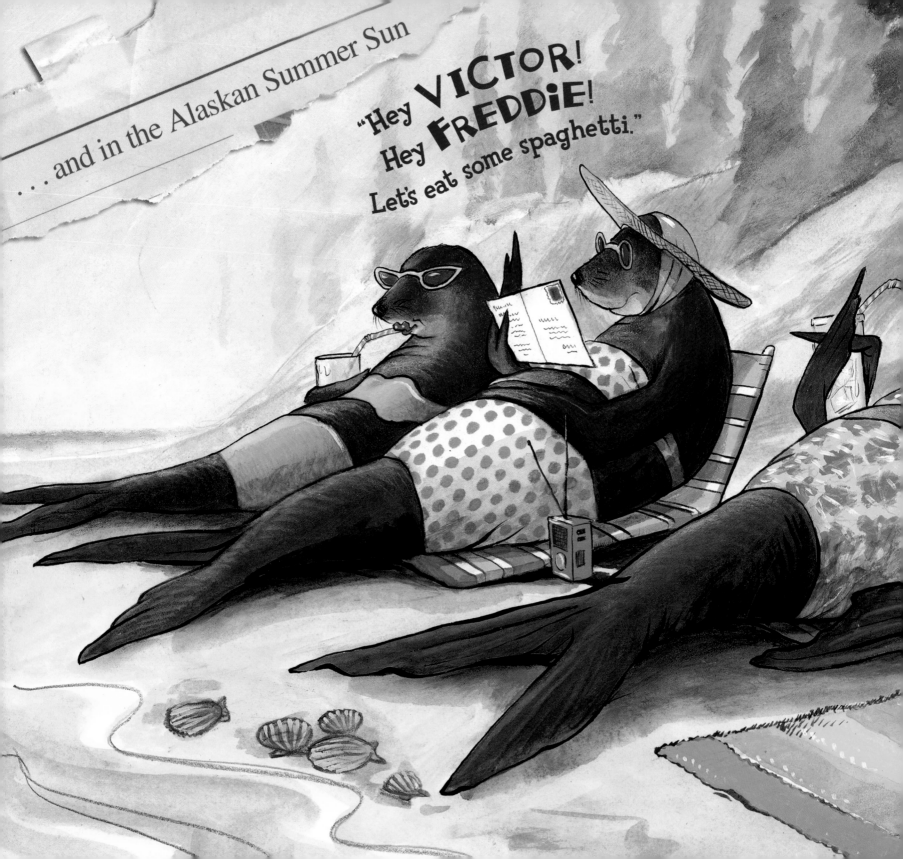

VICTOR VITO and FREDDIE VASCO

they like to eat slow. They never eat fast.

Oh, they ate their rice. They ate their beans.

They ate their rutabagas,

and they ate their collard greens.

They ate their rutabagas, and they ate their collard greens.

VICTOR VITO

Verse 1

Vic - tor Vi - to and Fred - die Vas - co ate a bur - ri - to with Ta - bas - co. They

put it on their rice. They put it on their beans, on ___ their ru - ta - ba - gas, and on ___ their col - lard greens. Hey,

Refrain

Vic - tor! (Hey, Vic - tor!) Hey, Fred - die (Hey, Fred - die!) Let's eat some (Let's eat some) spa - ghet - ti. (spa - ghet - ti.) Hey,

Vic - tor! (Hey, Vic - tor!) I'm read - y (I'm read - y) to eat some spa - ghet - ti with Fred - die.

Verse 2

Victor Vito and Freddie Vasco
moved from El Cerrito all the way to Alaska,
Oh they ate their rice. They ate their beans.
They ate their rutabagas,
and they ate their collard greens.

Refrain

Verse 3 (modulates to F)

Victor Vito and Freddie Vasco
they like to eat slow. They never eat fast.
Oh, they ate their rice. They ate their beans.
They ate their rutabagas,
and they ate their collard greens.

Refrain

Verse 4 (modulates back to E)

Victor Vito and Freddie Vasco
they like to eat fast. They never eat slow.
Oh, they ate their rice. They ate their beans.
They ate their rutabagas,
and they ate their collard greens.

Refrain 2 Times

P
BER

For Brian, with lots of love and collard greens. —L. B.

To Ken, with affection. —H. C.

07 08

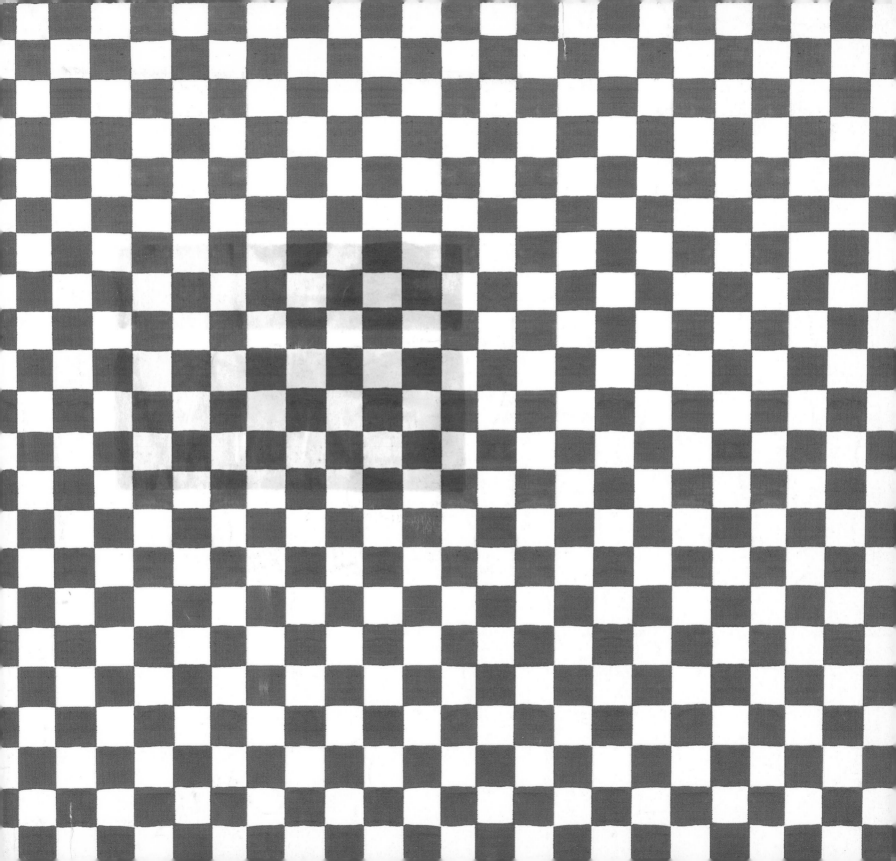

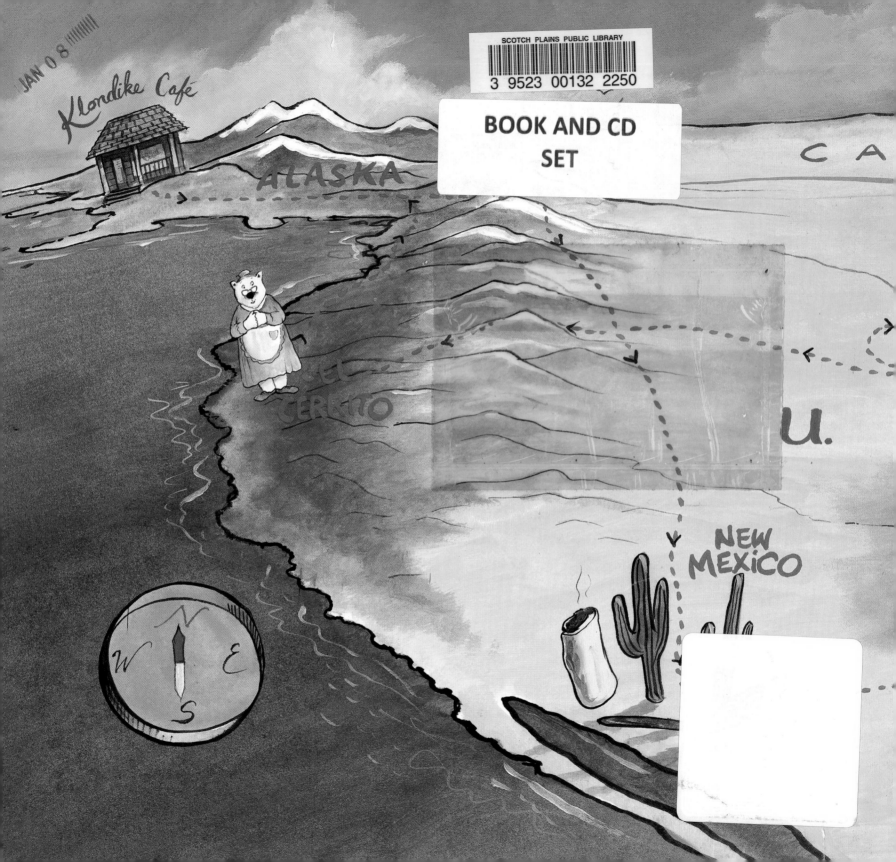